Schroom
By JNR

One night,

a tiny mushroom

began to grow

and grow,

and grow.

Schroom was a dreamer,

always dreaming of doing far out things

and going to far out places

He imagined floating away

on a puffy white cloud

for so long

it started to rain.

Luckily,

there are plenty of balloons about

to take him to

pink lollipop world

for his play date with the crown jewels.

He will take an adventure
inside the
reddest ruby

and go hiking within an emerald.

Perhaps,

he should go kayaking in the Amazon 

and find an amethyst bigger than him.

He can paddle to the sideways enchanted forest

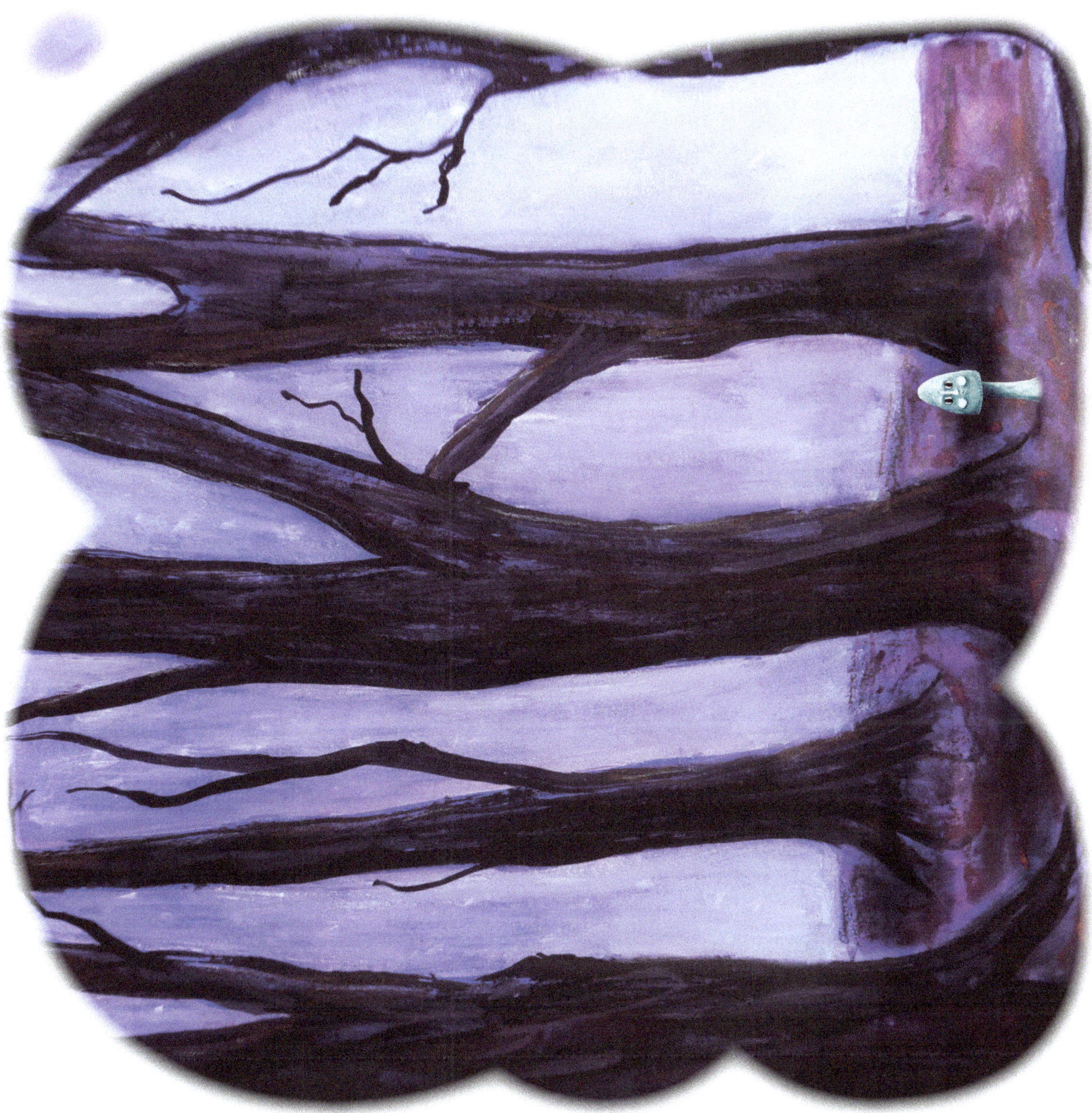

and be sideways

in a right-way-up

enchanted forest.

Then he'll go to the frog tuxedo party

except,

he can't...

because today,

he *is* kayaking

with his *new* friend Mischa.